Whoo Goes There?

JENNIFER A. ERICSSON   **ILLUSTRATED BY BERT KITCHEN**

A NEAL PORTER BOOK

ROARING BROOK PRESS

NEW YORK

Text copyright © 2009 by Jennifer A. Ericsson

Illustrations copyright © 2009 by Bert Kitchen

A Neal Porter Book

Published by Roaring Brook Press

Roaring Brook Press is a division of Holtzbrinck Publishing Holdings Limited Partnership

175 Fifth Avenue, New York, New York 10010

www.roaringbrookpress.com

Distributed in Canada by H. B. Fenn and Company, Ltd.

Cataloging-in-Publication Data is on file at the Library of Congress

ISBN-13: 978-1-59643-371-7

ISBN-10: 1-59643-371-X

Roaring Brook Press books are available for special promotions and premiums.

For details, contact: Director of Special Markets, Holtzbrinck Publishers.

First Edition October 2009

Book design by Jennifer Browne

Printed in China

2   4   6   8   10   9   7   5   3   1

In loving memory of my mother,
Eileen McAuliffe Barber
—J.A.E.

For my grandson, Ben
—B.K.

Owl sat on a branch of a tall tree. All was dark. All was quiet. Owl was hungry. He waited and watched with his big, round eyes.

Rustle, rustle.

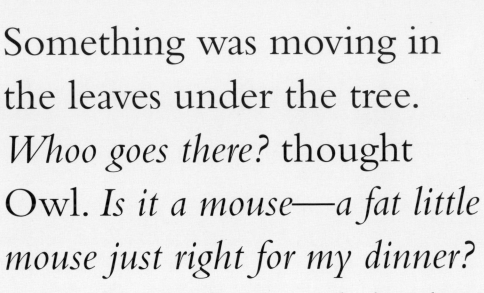

Something was moving in the leaves under the tree. *Whoo goes there?* thought Owl. *Is it a mouse—a fat little mouse just right for my dinner?* Owl waited and watched with his big, round eyes.

It was not a mouse. It was a cat. Owl watched the cat pad softly across the yard. He watched her slink around the side of the house. Owl did not want cat for his dinner.

Crack! Crack!

Something was moving under a bush. *Whoo goes there?* thought Owl. *Is it a squirrel—a fat little squirrel just right for my dinner?* Owl waited and watched with his big, round eyes.

It was not a squirrel. It was a skunk. Owl watched the skunk waddle out from under a bush. He saw the white stripe running down her back. Owl did not want skunk for his dinner.

Thump, thump.

Something was jumping through the grass.

Whoo goes there? thought Owl. *Is it a rabbit—a fat little rabbit just right for my dinner?* Owl waited and watched with his big, round eyes.

It was a rabbit. But chasing the rabbit was a fox. Owl watched the fox chase the rabbit. Rabbit would not be Owl's dinner tonight.

Eeeek, eeeek.

Something was flying through the air.
Whoo goes there? thought Owl. *Is it a*
bird—a fat little bird just
right for my dinner? Owl
waited and watched with
his big, round eyes.

It was not a bird. It was a bat. Owl watched the bat zig and zag across the sky. He felt tiny ripples in the air as she flew close to his tree. Owl did not want bat for his dinner.

Shuffle, shuffle.

Something was coming through the underbrush. *Whoo goes there?* thought Owl. *Is it an opossum—a fat little opossom just right for my dinner?* Owl waited and watched with his big, round eyes.

It was not an opossum. It was a porcupine. Owl watched her plod past his tree. He saw her sharp, pointy quills. Owl did not want porcupine for his dinner.

Splash, splash.

Something was moving down at the pond. *Whoo goes there?* thought Owl. Is *it a fish—a fat little fish just right for my dinner?* Owl waited and watched with his big, round eyes.

It was not a fish. It was a beaver. Owl watched the beaver glide across the pond. *Slap! Slap!* went his tail on the water. Owl did not want beaver for his dinner.

Skitter, skitter.

Whoo goes there? thought Owl.
It MUST *be a mouse—*
a fat little mouse just right
for my dinner.

And it *was* a mouse!
Owl spread his wings. He
swooped down to catch
his dinner, but . . .

Crash! Crash!

"Who goes there?"
called the man.

But no one was there.
All was dark. All was quiet.
Owl was gone.

And the mouse?

He was still searching
for his *own* dinner.